]

MW00938355

When I first informed my 10-year-old that I had a new book for her to read for school, she let out a sigh combined with a look like, "Oh, great! . . . That means something I won't enjoy." Little did she know that an exciting journey awaited her. She began reading and within the first chapter informed me that she already loved the book! She was taken away into a world of adventure seeking to discover a mystery. . . .Thank you, Susan Kilbride, for the fantastic opportunity to teach my children about their rich heritage and to keep them excited about learning more.

Tammy Wollner, author of *Keeping His Way Pure*

My 11-year-old son, who has no desire to learn from a textbook about the pilgrims and memorize boring dates, eagerly read The Pilgrim Adventure. *A living book,* The Pilgrim Adventure *combines real facts with some fiction to make the subject more appealing.*

Tina from Newbeehomeschooler.com

The books deal with the facts of the period without bogging the children down with too many dates and other things that always seem to make history boring to children.

Anna-Marie from Life's Adventures

This series is great for kids who loved the Magic Tree House *series but are now looking for books targeted to slightly older children. Written for upper elementary-aged kids, this book includes two likable main characters who love history.*

Pamela from the Lavish Book Shelf

Susan knows what homeschoolers are looking for and delivers that in her books.
Heidi Johnson from Homeschool-how-to.com

Never mind the mind-numbing and biased textbooks to learn history. You and your children will learn more from reading Ms. Kilbride's books and be far more entertained as well.
Gail Nagasako, author of *Homeschooling Why and How*

You cannot go wrong with an adventure with Finn and Ginny!
Richele McFarlin from Families.com

Thank you Ms. Kilbride. This captivating book is a keeper to add to our early American time period.
Tina Robertson from New Beginnings

If you've never read the Our America Series *by home educator, Susan Kilbride, you are missing out on a profoundly rare literary treat. Using journals and historical documents, Susan skillfully recreates the atmosphere of early America with a touch of 21st century technology. . . . My kids, ages 15, 12 and 10 have really enjoyed this series. They come away learning something new without the drudgery of a dry text book. Already they are anticipating volume 5!*
Lisa from Tales of a Homeschool Family

Susan Kilbride wrote this series to provide parents and teachers with living books to teach history. With short, manageable chapters and a captivating storyline, my younger boys were hooked right away and could not wait to find out what was going to happen next. . . .
Anne Campbell of the Home Educating Family Association

Our America. . .
The Pioneer Adventure

For some free activities to accompany this
book, visit the author's website at
http://funtasticunitstudies.com/

Other Books by Susan Kilbride

Science Unit Studies for Homeschoolers and Teachers

How to Teach about Electricity for Ages 8-13
(A Kindle eBook)

The Our America Series

The Pilgrim Adventure

The King Philip's War Adventure

The Salem Adventure

The Revolutionary War Adventure

The Pioneer Adventure

Our America. . .

The Pioneer Adventure

Susan Kilbride

Funtastic Unit Studies
USA

http://funtasticunitstudies.com/

Our America. . .
The Pioneer Adventure

Copyright © 2014 by Susan Kilbride

The drawing on the front cover is titled "Arkansas Pilgrims" by Paul Frenzeny and Jules Tavernier from "Sketches in the Far West," *Harper's Weekly* 1874.

Distributors and retailers can purchase this book directly from the publisher at:
www.createspace.com/info/createspacedirect

ISBN-13: 978-1499778373
ISBN-10: 1499778376

Acknowledgements

I would like to thank all of the reviewers who have encouraged me and supported this series over the past few years. Not only have you helped get the word out about my books, your kind words have inspired me to keep writing. I'd also like to thank my editor, Ellen Barski, whose corrections and suggestions have made me a better writer. And finally, I'd like to thank my family. You are my anchor.

The pioneers had to face many difficulties and endure untold hardships in building up an empire where those of later generations may live in peace and plenty.

John G. Abbott, who lost both parents and a grandfather on the Oregon Trail

Prologue
(For Newcomers to the Series)[a]

A year and a half before this story starts, twins Finn and Ginny were with their parents at their Uncle Peter and Aunt Martha's cabin home in Wisconsin. Things were going well and everyone was having a wonderful time—until one day Finn and Ginny woke up to find their parents missing. They had vanished without a trace.

Well, not quite. Uncle Peter knew what had happened. Uncle Peter was a physicist, and he had invented a time machine to help him learn about United States history. That evening he had taken it out to show Finn and Ginny's parents, but one thing led to another and he never got around to showing it to them. Instead, he accidentally left the remote control for the time machine on the coffee table in the living room.

The next morning Finn and Ginny's parents woke early and picked up the remote in the living room to turn on the TV. Only instead of turning

---

[a] Most of this is covered in *The Pilgrim Adventure*

on the TV, they turned on the time machine. Uncle Peter came downstairs and found the time machine remote laying on the floor and no sign of Finn and Ginny's parents. They were gone, and only Uncle Peter knew what had happened. For a year, Uncle Peter secretly ventured back in time to try to rescue Finn and Ginny's parents, but so far he hasn't found them.

As for Finn and Ginny, they were distraught. They had no idea what had happened to their parents. For months, they both had constant nightmares and couldn't bear to be parted from each other. As time went on, they became more accustomed to the situation, but their missing parents were never far from their minds.

One day, about a year after their parents' disappearance, Finn saw Uncle Peter vanish in front of his eyes, only to walk into the room a few minutes later. When Finn and Ginny confronted him, asking if that was how their parents had disappeared, Uncle Peter admitted he knew what had happened to their parents. He told Finn and Ginny about the time machine.

Finn and Ginny secretly decided to use the time machine to search for their parents themselves. At the time this story opens, Finn and Ginny are twelve, and they've already used the time machine four times. They've discovered some of the time machine's quirks, such as how they can't bring anything with them back in time and how their clothes are automatically changed into the proper clothes for the time period. One of the most interesting things the time machine does is to send them to places where their ancestors lived. But the strangest thing is that their ancestors know who they are—only they think Finn and Ginny belong in their time period. They don't know Finn and Ginny are from the future.

So, as the story opens, Finn and Ginny are about to go on another hunt for their missing parents. . . .

1

Another Try

Ginny sighed as she wiped the last dish. "I feel as if we've been doing chores forever!" she complained.

"You're not kidding!" agreed Finn. "Aunt Martha sure is keeping us busy. I wanted to play a game on the computer and I haven't had a chance all day."

"And I still have some math problems to finish. It seems as if we never have fun anymore," said Ginny.

"It's times like these that I really miss Mom and Dad," grumbled Finn.

Ginny stopped what she was doing and looked at him. "Mom and Dad made us do chores, too. Or did you forget having to help paint all of our bedrooms?"

"You're right," said Finn sheepishly. "I guess

I'm just in a bad mood because we haven't found Mom and Dad yet. After all the adventures and dangers we've been through, it seems as if we should have found them by now."

"Well, we have to keep on trying. I'm not ready to give up," Ginny said fiercely.

"Of course not! In fact, let's try again the next chance we get."

"Aunt Martha and Uncle Peter are going out tonight. That would be the perfect time," suggested Ginny.

"Sounds good to me," said Finn with a grin.

* * * *

That evening, after Aunt Martha and Uncle Peter had gone out, the twins dug in Uncle Peter's dresser and found the time machine remote he kept hidden in a sock.

"Don't forget to check the batteries," reminded Ginny. "We don't want the same problems we had last time."

"They look fine. Uncle Peter must have changed them," replied Finn.

The twins sat down on the floor with the remote in front of them.

"I hope we don't find ourselves in another war this time," said Ginny nervously. "I've had enough of wars to last a lifetime."

"Wherever we go, I hope it's not winter," said Finn. "And that we find Mom and Dad!"

"Maybe this will be the trip we find them," Ginny said hopefully. She grabbed Finn's hand and pushed the button on the remote. Her stomach dropped as the world started spinning. Then everything went blurry and the twins were pulled back in time.

2

The Wagon Train

"Finn! Ginny! Hurry! We don't want them to leave without us!" a woman yelled.

Finn opened his eyes. He and Ginny were sitting under a tree next to a road full of covered wagons. People bustled around tending to their horses, grabbing wayward children, loading last-minute items into their wagons, and generally getting in each other's way. He shook his head to clear it from the confusion around him.

Ginny tucked the time remote into the pocket of her dress as she surveyed the scene. "Finn, I think we're in pioneer times, sometime in the 1800s. Look at the clothes. Don't they look like something out of 'Little House on the Prairie'? And look at the covered wagons! Wouldn't it be fun to travel in one?"

Finn stood and helped Ginny to her feet.

"Well, that woman over there is calling us. If she's one of our ancestors, it looks as if you might get your wish."

The woman gestured to them from across the road. "Hurry up! Your Uncle Alexander doesn't want to be last in line. Finn, you take the smaller wagon. Ginny can ride with you. Just follow your uncle's wagon and you'll do just fine."

Finn warily eyed the wagon with its two oxen warily. "Boy, am I glad we rode on wagons during our Revolutionary War adventure," he whispered. "But I've never driven a wagon with oxen."

"You'll figure it out. It can't be all that different than horses," Ginny said optimistically as they climbed onto the front of the wagon "But who is Uncle Alexander? We don't want to follow the wrong wagon!"

"He must be the man driving the wagon the woman just climbed into," said Finn. It's right in front of us—the one with four oxen instead of two."

"Let's hope you're right," said Ginny as Finn pulled on the reins to move the oxen team onto the road to follow the woman's wagon. Luckily, the oxen followed his directions.

"I wonder where we're going?" Finn said.

"Wherever it is, you've got your wish. It's not winter," said Ginny. "It looks like early spring."

"And you've got yours. We're not in the middle of a war! Maybe this adventure will be easier than some of the others we've been on. Did you check the time remote to see how long we're going to be here?"

"Yes, it says we'll be here 153 days."

"That should give us plenty of time to search for Mom and Dad. And since it looks as if we'll be traveling, we can search for them as we go along."

Ginny glanced around them. "There are about thirty wagons in this train."

"Train? What do you mean, train?" asked Finn.

"This is called a wagon train," explained Ginny. "The settlers moving west would travel together in groups called trains. They figured they would be safer from Indian attacks if they traveled together instead of separately. They would vote on a captain to lead the train. He was usually someone who had traveled west before."

"Where did you learn all of this?" asked Finn.

"In books. Remember when I was interested in the pioneers last year?"

"Oh yeah, I forgot about your pioneer phase," replied Finn. "Well, maybe all that reading you did will help us here."

Ginny chewed her lip. She was starting to remember all of the dangers the pioneers had encountered. "We might need all of the help we can get."

3

Nooning

"Whoa!" called Finn as he pulled back on the reins.

"I wonder why we're stopping?" asked Ginny.

"Well, it's about lunchtime. Maybe we're stopping to eat."

Ahead of them, the man they had guessed was Uncle Alexander jumped down from his wagon and walked back to them. He had a cheerful face with a dark mustache and goatee.

"Well, Finn and Ginny, how are you enjoying your first day on the trail?"

"Very exciting, sir," said Ginny. "Thank you for letting us travel with you."

"It's we who should be thanking you! Because of your help, we don't need to hire someone to drive the second wagon. Your Aunt Eleanor grew up in New York and hasn't spent a lot of time in the country. She isn't that comfortable driving the wagon, plus she needs to have her hands free to take care of the children."

Ginny's face brightened. "Uncle Alexander, could I learn how to drive a wagon, too?" she asked hopefully.

"That's a great idea!" he replied as he helped her down from the wagon. "Pioneer women need to learn these kinds of skills, and it would be nice for Finn to have a break from driving once in a while."

"Did you hear that, Finn? I'm going to learn how to drive the wagon!" she whispered. "I think I'm going to like this period in time!"

Finn gave her a quick grin. He knew how frustrated she'd been in their past adventures always having to do the "girl" jobs.

"We're going to be here for a few hours until it cools down," said Uncle Alexander. "We'll be doing this every day to give the teams a rest. Captain John, the leader of our train, calls it 'nooning.' While we're here, we'll unyoke the oxen so they can do some grazing. Ginny, you can help unyoke them and then help harness them again when it's time to leave. If you're going to learn how to drive a team, you need to learn how to yoke them to the wagon.

"Yes, sir!" replied Ginny with a big smile.

* * * *

After Finn and Ginny helped Uncle Alexander with the oxen, they went over to where Aunt Eleanor was cooking over a fire. The sound of a baby wailing came from inside the wagon.

"Ginny, could you help your cousin Mary watch the little girls for me while I finish this stew? And Finn, could you help your uncle fill that barrel with water from the spring? The spring is over in those reeds."

While Finn went with his uncle, Ginny climbed into the wagon to meet her new cousins. She saw a dark-haired girl about ten years old frantically trying to calm a screaming baby.

"Would you like me to hold her?" asked Ginny.

"Oh, yes! Please!" said the girl in relief as she handed the squalling baby to Ginny.

Ginny bounced the baby in her lap as she looked around the wagon. Three little faces stared up at her from a corner.

"Are you our cousin Ginny?" asked one of the girls.

The baby seemed to calm down a bit as Ginny said, "Yes, I am. And what are your names?"

"I'm Lillian and she's Marion. We're twins," the little girl said proudly.

"I'm a twin, too!" said Ginny. "Only my twin is a boy, my brother Finn." She turned to the other little girl. "And what is your name?"

"I'm Catherine. I'm eight," she said. "The baby's name is Jessie and my big sister is Mary."

"Things have happened so quickly, I don't

even know where we are going," said Ginny.

"We're going to Nebraska," said Mary. "Papa's going to buy us a farm to live on. He says it will take about ten days to get there."

"Is everyone in this wagon train going to Nebraska?" asked Ginny.

"No, most of them are going to Oregon or California, but Papa doesn't want to go that far. So we're stopping in Nebraska at a place called Camp Creek. Will you be staying with us?"

"I don't know yet," said Ginny. "I need to talk to my brother first."

* * * *

Later that afternoon, after they had harnessed the oxen and were on the trail again, Ginny brought the question up to Finn. "Uncle Alexander is stopping in Nebraska, and the rest of the wagon train is going to keep traveling west. I was thinking maybe we should go west with them. That way we can cover more area looking for Mom and Dad."

"I think that's a good idea," said Finn. "We haven't had much luck looking for them in the east. Maybe we'll have better luck in the west. I'll ask around to see if there is another family we can ride with after Uncle Alexander's family leaves the wagon train."

4

The Train Moves On

Ten days later, Finn and Ginny waved good-bye to Uncle Alexander and Aunt Eleanor as they stood in front of the land where they were going to make their new home.

"Don't forget," called Uncle Alexander, "if you ever need a place to stay, you can always visit the Bains of Camp Creek!"

"Thank you!" called Finn. "We won't forget!" He gave the reins a shake and the wagon went on its way. The twins were now driving another team of oxen for the Campbell family, whose other driver had decided to stay in Nebraska to start a homestead. Mr. and Mrs. Campbell and their baby were riding in one wagon while Finn and Ginny drove the other.

"I'm starting to feel like an old hand at this," said Finn as he urged the wagon forward.

"Yes, we're really pioneers now!" exclaimed Ginny. "Though so far not much has happened. It's been just like camping in our own time, only with horses and wagons instead of cars to get us from campsite to campsite."

"Well, I think we're on the more populated part of the trail. I hear it gets wilder the farther west we go."

"I'm actually getting a little bored riding in a wagon all day," admitted Ginny.

"Me too," said Finn. "But at least we're traveling through different places so we can look for Mom and Dad as we go. It's better than being stuck in one town."

"Still, I wish something would happen," said Ginny. "This is going to be a long, boring adventure if all we're doing is riding in a wagon for five months."

Little did she know that she would soon regret those words.

5

Crossing a River

Finn and Ginny looked with dismay at the sight in front of them. The Elkhorn River had flooded and there was water everywhere for miles. The wagons waited in a line for the ferry to take them across, but the ferry wasn't running. The captain called for a halt and everyone set up camp where they were and prepared to wait for the ferry to start again.

* * * *

Four days later, they were still waiting.

* * * *

Seven days later, they were still waiting.

* * * *

On the eighth day, the captain called everyone from the train together for a meeting. "We can't afford to wait much longer." he said. "Otherwise we won't make it to Oregon before winter comes. I suggest we build our own raft and ferry the wagons over ourselves."

The settlers agreed. They were all tired of waiting for the ferry to start again. The men got to work building a raft and three days later they were ready to start across the river.

It was pouring rain. Finn and Ginny stood with the others around the captain to hear their last-minute instructions. Water dripped off of hats and beards as the captain spoke. Like many of the travelers, Ginny and Finn wore gutta-percha ponchos to keep dry.[b]

"First, we'll ferry everyone to that large island in the middle of the river," he said. "We'll test the raft by poling it across empty to the island with some of the men. There will be a rope tied on each end of the raft. Some of the men will stay on the island so they can use the rope to pull the raft to the island when it is loaded. We'll have other men on the shore to pull it back and to help load the wagons and cattle."

Finn was helping the men pull the raft back and forth so Ginny had to ferry their oxen by herself. She unharnessed the team and watched

---

[b] A poncho made from muslin cloth soaked in latex made from the sap of a Gutta-percha tree.

as their wagon was hauled over to the island. When the raft returned, she carefully led the oxen onto the raft, and the captain handed her some cloth to cover their eyes. "This should help keep them calm," he said.

"What about keeping *me* calm?" asked Ginny with a grin.

The captain laughed. "If you like, I can give you a cloth, too."

"No, thank you. I think I'd prefer to be able to see what's happening if the raft sinks," Ginny replied. Despite her jokes, Ginny was nervous as she stood next to the oxen. The men started pulling on the rope and she braced her feet, clinging to the ox next to her. The rain poured down and, even with her poncho, she was wet and cold when the raft finally made it to the island.

"Go ahead and let the oxen loose so they can graze," the captain said. "It's too late to ferry the rest of the way to the other side of the river, so once everyone is on the island we'll camp here for the night. Don't unpack anything. Just stay in your wagon. We want to be ready to move out as soon as it's light."

That night, Ginny and Finn had a hard time falling asleep. Thunder crashed and the night was lit by lightning. The rain poured down so hard that it seeped through the canvas on the wagon, and they had to sleep with their ponchos on. Finally, after what seemed like hours, they managed to fall asleep.

6

Flood!

"**W**e are all lost! We are all lost!" The mournful wail rolled through the dark camp. Finn and Ginny sat up and looked at each other.

"Who do you think is making that awful noise?" Ginny exclaimed.

"Let's see what's going on," said Finn as he climbed out of his bed roll and jumped out of the wagon.

Splash!

"Wait, Ginny! Don't jump! We're completely surrounded by water! The island is flooded!"

Ginny grabbed a lantern and poked her head out of the wagon. As she raised the lantern over her head, she could see that much of the island was underwater. The rain was still pouring down. "We'd better get out of here quickly!" she shouted. "Before we all get washed downstream!"

Lightning flashed and was followed by the roar of thunder. Through the gloom, Ginny could see the captain trying to calm old Mr. Ames, the man who had been wailing. Then the captain turned and shouted, "Everyone wake up! We've got to get out of here!"

Men began to jump out of the wagons at the captain's warning shouts.

"Quick, men! Grab the raft and pull it over to the side where the water is still low. Start loading the first wagon!" shouted the captain.

"But that's the side we just came from!" yelled one of the men. "We'll be going backwards!"

"There's too much water on the other side of the island," explained the captain. "We won't be able to load the wagons onto the raft. And the shore is much farther away on that side. We need to get everyone to safety immediately!"

Some of the men ran over and pushed the first wagon onto the raft. Then Finn jumped on the raft with a group of men and they quickly poled the raft to shore. They unloaded the wagon and the men who remained on the island pulled the raft back with the rope and started loading the next wagon. After several hours and a lot of hard work, they managed to get everyone back to safety.

"But what about the cattle?" asked Ginny. "They're still trapped on the island!"

"They were too spooked," said Finn wearily. "We couldn't get them onto the raft. We had to leave them on the island."

The sun was just starting to rise when the twins heard cattle bellowing. The twins ran with a group of settlers to the shoreline to see what was wrong. The cattle were frantically running back and forth along the only part of the island that wasn't covered in water. Suddenly, first an ox, then a cow plunged into the swift water. They were followed by the whole herd. The settlers watched in horror as the cattle were quickly swept downstream.

"They're all going to drown!" cried Ginny. "How will we pull our wagons?"

Finn pulled his boots back on. "We'd better follow them to see if they make it to shore," he said. He jumped out of the wagon into ankle-deep mud and walked over to the captain. "Sir, would you like me to try to track them to see if we can find them?"

Ginny splashed over to them. "If you're going, then I'm going too," she declared.

"I'll organize a party of men to search for the cattle," said the captain. "You two are welcome to go along."

An hour later, after slogging through ankle-deep mud, they found the cattle safe and sound. All of the people and animals were now safe on shore.

But they were still on the wrong side of the river.

7

More Danger

Eight long days later, the water had receded and the settlers decided to try to cross the river again.

The captain called everyone together. "The water has subsided enough that we won't need the raft for the second part of the crossing. We'll ferry the wagons and teams to the island on the raft. Then we'll hitch the oxen to the wagons and ford the river to the other shore. I've already forded it myself and stuck some sticks in the river where the deep holes are, so whatever you do, steer away from those sticks. Stay upriver from them and you should be able to cross safely."

Finn helped load the first ox team onto the raft. They were sending the oxen first because the island was so muddy they were going to have to use them to pull the wagons off the raft.

The captain's wagon was next. "Since I'm the one who set the ford markers, I'll lead the way," he said.

Finn and Ginny continued loading wagons and oxen on the raft until it was time for them to take their wagon across to the island. When they landed on the island, they could see the other wagons going back and forth across the ford. It was so muddy that people could only take half-loads, so the twins had to unload half of the items in their wagon and leave them on the island to be picked up later.

"Are you ready?" Finn asked Ginny. They had never forded a river before and this one was full of mud and high, fast water.

"Not really," said Ginny. "But what choice do I have? We can't stay on this island forever!" She grinned.

Finn looked at the other wagons on the far shore. "Well, if they can do it, so can we," he said as their oxen plunged into the swirling river.

Ginny anxiously watched the oxen. "The waves are making it hard for them to keep their heads above water!"

"The current is pushing us toward the stakes!" Finn shouted. He pulled hard on the reins and managed to guide the team to the upriver side of the first stake.

Ginny turned to watch another team that was going back to the island for their second load. "Look! The men in that wagon aren't going the

right way!" she pointed. "They're going right toward the deep part of the river!" She shouted and
gestured to the men to keep to the high side of
the stakes, but they didn't notice her. The twins
watched in horror as the men's wagon lurched
into the deep part of the river and sank out of
sight.

Ginny gasped. "We've got to help them!"

"I don't know how!" said Finn, struggling with
the reins. "It's all I can do to keep our wagon
from falling in."

"Look, the men have managed to un-yoke
their oxen!" Ginny said. "Two of them are riding
them out!"

"Where's the third man?" asked Finn.

Ginny strained to see. "I don't know. Maybe
he's on the other side."

The twins managed to get to shore just in
time to see the captain helping the two young
men to land. "Where's Montgomery?" the captain
asked.

"He can swim and we can't," one of the young
men said. "When we sank, he told us we were
lost if we couldn't swim and he left us to our fate.
We stayed with the oxen and that saved us."

Finn and the captain ran to search for Montgomery. Farther downstream, they saw the
young man floating in the water. He had
drowned. Later, they found the wagon and pulled
it to shore. It took the rest of the day to get everyone to safety.

The next morning, they buried Montgomery. The captain said a prayer over the grave and one of the women led them all in a familiar hymn. This was the group's first death on the trail, and everyone was somber. Their eyes were opened to the dangers of the journey.

8

Injured!

"**H**ey, Finn! My dad is sending some of us ahead to scout the next river. Would you like to ride with us? He said you could use one of his horses."

Finn and Ginny had made friends with some of the other kids on the wagon train. One of them, Jim, was the captain's son. He was riding his horse alongside their wagon as he called to Finn.

Finn turned to Ginny who was next to him in the wagon. "Would you mind driving the wagon by yourself for a while?"

"Only if you agree to drive it later so I can visit with Sarah in her wagon," Ginny replied.

"It's a deal," said Finn with a grin as he handed the reins to her. He jumped down while the wagon was still moving and ran towards the first wagon in the train where the captain rode.

Ginny urged the oxen onward. It was going to be boring riding without Finn, but at least she could look forward to a visit with Sarah.

* * * *

An hour later the sound of pounding hooves shook Ginny from the half-daze she'd been in from riding so long.

"Ginny! Come quickly! Finn fell off his horse!" Jim yelled as he pulled up to the wagon.

Ginny hurriedly pulled the wagon to the side of the road. "What happened? Is Finn hurt?"

"A rattlesnake spooked his horse, and when it reared up Finn fell off and hit his head. He's unconscious!"

"Oh no! I've got to go to him right now!" exclaimed Ginny.

"You take my horse and I'll drive your wagon," said Jim. "He's about a mile ahead of the train. Samuel and Hank are with him."

Ginny hopped off the wagon and hauled herself up onto Jim's horse. "Thanks, Jim!" she yelled as she took off down the trail.

A few minutes later Ginny pulled up to where Finn was lying by the side of the road.

"Finn! Finn! Are you okay?" she cried.

Samuel, one of Finn's new friends, looked up from Finn's side. "I think he's coming around now."

Ginny threw herself next to her twin and grabbed his hand. "Finn, can you hear me?" she whispered with a sob.

Finn groaned and opened his eyes. "What happened? Why does my head hurt?" His voice was weak.

"You fell off your horse," said Samuel.

"My horse? I don't remember riding a horse," said Finn."

"You were helping us scout the river," said Hank. "Don't you remember?"

"No," said Finn. "He looked at Samuel and then Hank. "I don't even remember you." Then he turned his bleary gaze to Ginny. "And who are you? Why are you holding my hand?"

"Oh Finn! Don't you remember me? I'm your sister!" cried Ginny. She burst into tears.

9

Strangers

Samuel, Hank, and Jim helped Ginny make a bed in the back of the wagon and then they settled Finn into it. He seemed a bit shaken from the fall and hadn't spoken another word.

"There was a doctor in the train that left the campsite ahead of us this morning," said Jim. Sam and I are going to try to catch up to it to see if he will come back to look at Finn."

"That would be wonderful," said Ginny. "Thank you." The tears had dried on her face and she smiled bravely as the boys rode off. Then she shook the reins and urged the oxen forward. The wagon train couldn't afford to stop for one injured boy or they might get trapped in the mountains in the winter, and she didn't want to get separated from the train. As they began to move, she heard a weak voice behind her.

"Ginny?"

"Yes, Finn?"

"I'm sorry I don't remember you."

Ginny blinked back tears as she said, "Me, too. But hopefully you will start remembering things soon. What *do* you remember?"

"I don't remember anything. I don't remember who I am or who my parents are. And nothing here seems familiar. But why are we on a wagon train? Are we in a movie or something?"

Ginny paused. What should she tell him? She thought a moment and then said, "You're not going to believe this, but you and I are from the future, and we've gone back in time to find our lost parents."

Finn was silent. Then he said angrily, "You're right. I *don't* believe you. Stop making fun of me! It's not funny!"

Ginny looked over her shoulder at him. "I'm not making fun of you! It's true!"

"Well, I don't believe you. We must be in a movie."

"If we're in a movie, where are the movie cameras? The lights? There aren't any because we're not in a movie! We're back in time!"

"I think you should stop trying to fool me and take me to a hospital. In fact, you should have taken me to a hospital right away! Who are you people? Have you kidnapped me?"

"No, we haven't kidnapped you! I'm your sister and we *are* back in time, just like I said."

Finn groaned and lay back down. "Don't talk to me. My head hurts and I can't deal with this right now."

Ginny chewed her lip in silence. What was she going to do? How could she get Finn to believe her? And what was he going to say to the other people on the train?

* * * *

A little while later the doctor rode up with Samuel and Jim. Ginny pulled the wagon over so he could climb aboard to talk to Finn.

Finn glared at her. "Send her away! I don't want to talk when she's around!"

The doctor looked at Ginny with worried eyes and nodded. Ginny quietly climbed down from the wagon and stood off to the side with Samuel and Jim.

"What's wrong? Why is he mad at you?" asked Jim.

"He doesn't believe I'm his sister. He thinks we kidnapped him."

Jim stared. "Why does he think that?"

"Because everything seems strange to him. He doesn't think he belongs here."

Just then, the doctor climbed down from the wagon with a concerned expression on his face. "He's in pretty bad shape. He doesn't seem to remember anything and he's having delusions. He keeps talking about wanting something called a 'cell phone,' whatever that is. He's obviously very ill. Do you think you can handle him, Ginny?"

Ginny nodded. "Don't worry, doctor. I'll take care of him."

"I'll come back tonight to check on him," replied the doctor as he climbed back on his horse. "Try not to upset him. He needs quiet and rest to give him time to heal."

10

A Quiet Evening

Finn slept quietly for the rest of the day. They camped that night near the Little Blue River. Ginny decided that Finn would be more comfortable if she slept in a tent by herself than in the wagon with him. She borrowed one from the Campbells when she went to get the stew for their supper.

"How's Finn doing?" asked Mrs. Campbell as she handed Ginny the stew.

"He doesn't remember me or anyone," said Ginny sadly. "I don't know what to do to help him."

"I don't think there is much you can do," said Mrs. Campbell. "Just make sure he rests and gets plenty of food. What he needs most is time to heal. I'm sure he will recover his memory eventually," she said reassuringly.

"Thank you. I hope you're right," said Ginny as she walked back to her wagon.

Finn was still laying down when Ginny peered through the wagon flap. "I've brought you some food," she said. "Do you feel well enough to eat?"

Finn slowly sat up, wincing as he moved. "Yes. I feel like I haven't eaten for a week," he said as he took the bowl. "I think I've figured out what's going on here. You folks are reenactors and you're reenacting a wagon train. That's why everyone always stays in character." He paused as he took another bite. "What I don't get is why you've kidnapped me."

Ginny thought quickly. *He won't believe we're back in time. Maybe if I agree with him, he'll calm down until he regains his memory. Otherwise, I'm afraid he'll try to run away and that could get him killed.*

"That's exactly right," she said aloud. "We're reenactors. And you're one too—that's why you're with us. We didn't kidnap you. You really are my brother."

Finn smiled in relief. "And I suppose you thought it was funny to tell me we'd gone back in time."

"Yeah," said Ginny with a sigh, "real funny."

"Well that makes sense at least. How long will we be with this wagon train?"

"About four months," said Ginny. "That should be plenty of time for you to regain your memory."

"I sure hope so," said Finn. "I don't like not remembering anything." He turned his head. "What's that sound?"

"Some of the men are playing fiddle music. If you like, we can walk over there to listen. I don't think you should dance though. The doctor said you should rest."

Finn shook his head and then winced. "I think I'll pass tonight. My head still hurts."

Mrs. Campbell peered through the wagon flap. "Finn, how are you doing? Do you need anything?"

Finn looked bewildered. "I'm sorry. I don't know who you are."

Ginny reached over and patted Finn's hand. "Finn, this is Mrs. Campbell. She and her husband own the wagon we're riding in." She turned to Mrs. Campbell. "Thank you for checking on us. I think we're fine for now. Finn is feeling a bit better and should be able to travel tomorrow."

"Oh good, we've been very worried. We don't want the jostling of the wagon to make him worse.

Finn smiled at her. "I'm sure I'll be up and about by tomorrow. Thank you for your kindness."

As she walked away, he turned to Ginny. "I don't remember how to drive a wagon. Can you show me?"

"No problem. It's actually pretty easy," said Ginny. "I can also show you how to harness the oxen." She yawned. "I think I'm going to turn in now. It's been a long day."

"Goodnight."

11

A Scare

"Do you see that rider up ahead?" asked Finn. "He's tearing along the trail toward us as if a ghost were after him."

The train had been traveling for a couple of hours. Finn was feeling better and was riding up front with Ginny.

"I wonder what he wants?" Ginny said. "He must be coming from a train ahead of ours."

The twins watched as the rider stopped at the captain's wagon and started gesturing wildly.

Suddenly, the captain called out, "Corral the wagons! Corral the wagons!"

Finn and Ginny looked at each other. "What does that mean?" asked Finn.

"Uncle Alexander told me that as we get closer to hostile Indian territory we'd be corralling the wagons every night. The wagons are put into a circle so that the people and cattle can shelter inside it."

"Do you think there's going to be an Indian attack?" asked Finn.

"I don't know," said Ginny with a frown. "No one has seemed too worried about it until now."

The wagons ahead of them began to form a circle. As they approached them, the captain rushed up.

"Finn! Ginny! A wagon train ahead of us was just attacked by Indians and a band of about three hundred warriors is headed our way." He pointed to their right. "Put your wagon over there and line it up like the others. Unyoke your oxen and lead them inside the wagon corral. Then stay in there with them."

Finn and Ginny quickly did as they were told and pulled their oxen toward the center of the circle. Women and children milled all around them. One woman started wailing.

"They're going to kill us! We'll all be scalped!"

Children cried and some people began praying. Ginny started to shake.

"Oh Finn! It's just like when I was captured by Indians!"[c]

Finn looked at her strangely. "Don't you think you're taking this a bit too seriously? I mean it's only a reenactment after all. No one is really going to get hurt."

---

[c] *The King Philip's War Adventure*

Ginny froze in place. Finn had been acting so normally that she'd forgotten he had amnesia. She was going to have to keep a close eye on him to make sure he didn't get hurt. If he didn't believe the bullets and arrows were real, he might do something crazy and get himself killed.

She faked a laugh. "Well, it all seems so real, doesn't it? And since we're here, we might as well play along."

The wailing grew louder and then the captain strode angrily over. "Quiet down! You can't show any fear! If you scream and cry we'll be attacked for sure!"

The noise died down and Finn grinned. "Thank goodness! I don't think I could have taken much more of that."

Just as the last wagon pulled into the corral, they saw a cloud of dust coming toward them. And then three hundred Indian warriors on horseback rushed at them, yipping like coyotes and waving their weapons.

The captain ordered the men with rifles to form a line. "Keep cool men! And do not fire until I say to!"

When the Indians were about fifty feet away, the captain stepped out in front of them and raised his hand palm out. He pushed it forward and back a few times.

The Indians looked at him and looked at the line of men. They looked at each other and then wheeled their horses and rode away.

Ginny heaved a huge sigh of relief and slumped against Finn.

"Well that was a bit of a let-down!" exclaimed Finn. "I thought for sure we'd have some kind of fire-fight. I wonder where they found so many reenactors?"

"Hush, Finn," whispered Ginny. "You're getting out of character."

"Sorry," Finn whispered back. "I'm still not used to all of this. Did you notice how the wagons are pulled up? It's not how they do it in the movies."

"You're right, it's not in a simple circle like in the movies—the wagons are more overlapped. This way seems more protected," said Ginny.

After waiting a bit to make sure the Indians were really gone, the train re-formed and started moving forward. After a while they came upon the train that had been attacked.

The captain called for a halt, and people climbed down from their wagons to help however they could.

Finn looked wide-eyed at the scene in front of them. Three children lay on the ground crying as the doctor bound their wounds. A woman sat with tears running down her face while her husband held her hand.

"Boy, this sure looks real," he said. "These folks are good actors!"

Ginny shushed him.

The captain came over to them. "Will you kids

help round up their loose animals? The Indians stampeded most of them, but their captain says there's enough left to pull their wagons."

For the next hour, Finn and Ginny helped with the animals, and soon the two trains were on their way again. And from that day on, they formed a corral with their wagons every night.

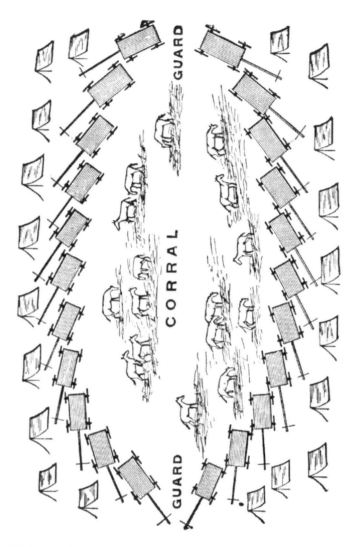

Taken from *The History of Utah, 1540-1886*
By Hubert Howe Bancroft (1889)

12

Cholera

Finn reached for another piece of buttered bread, but then he stopped and looked at it. "How did we get butter?" he whispered. "Has someone been sneaking out to a grocery store at night?"

Ginny laughed. "No, Mrs. Campbell milks their cow every evening, and in the morning she skims off the cream and puts it into the butter churn. The churn is tied to the wagon and the rocking of the wagon churns the cream, so by evening we have butter. You'd better enjoy it though. I hear that as we go farther west it's harder to find grass for the cows, and they may not produce any more milk."

Just then the captain called for the wagons to get in line, so the twins packed their food and climbed aboard.

A few miles later, Ginny nudged Finn. "Look

at that! There must be hundreds of tents lined along the river. It's like a tent city!"

"I still can't believe how many reenactors they've found for this tour," remarked Finn. "How much did we pay for this trip? It must have cost a fortune to organize."

Ginny shifted uneasily. "I don't know." As she peered ahead, she saw the captain slow down to talk to a man on the side of the road. The captain gave a start of surprise and then hurriedly nodded as he urged his team forward. The other wagons followed. Ginny stared at the tents as they drove by. Sallow faces peered out at her.

"These people look sick," said Finn. "Do you think something is wrong?"

"It sure looks like it," replied Ginny. "We'll probably hear about it when we stop for nooning."

* * * *

"Did you hear?" Mrs. Campbell asked them when they walked over to her wagon during the nooning. "Cholera! All of those people on the side of the river had cholera! That's why we didn't stop at Fort Kearney. The captain didn't want to risk any one from our train catching it."

"What's cholera?" asked Ginny.

"What's cholera? Why, it's a horrible disease that causes severe diarrhea. There are people who caught it in the morning and died by nightfall!" exclaimed Mrs. Campbell.

"Well, I'm glad the captain didn't stop," said Ginny. "I hope no one on our train catches it."

But her hopes were unanswered. That night a man from the train died of the disease.

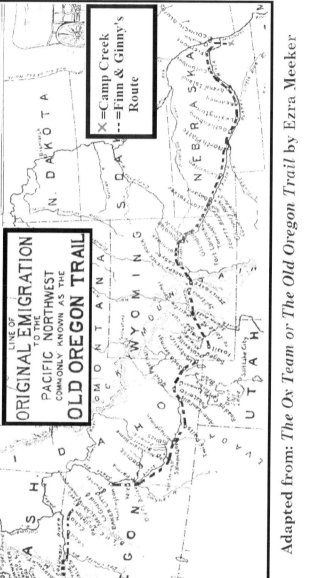

Legend:
X = Camp Creek
--- = Finn & Ginny's Route

LINE OF
ORIGINAL EMIGRATION
TO THE
PACIFIC NORTHWEST
COMMONLY KNOWN AS THE
OLD OREGON TRAIL

Adapted from: *The Ox Team or The Old Oregon Trail* by Ezra Meeker

13

Runaway

Finn glanced sideways at Ginny as he held the reins. Then he pounded his knee in frustration.

"Are you okay?" asked Ginny.

"I just wish I could remember something! I can't remember you, I can't remember our parents, and I can't remember where I live. What if I never get my memory back?"

Ginny chewed on her lower lip. "I'm sure everything will eventually come back to you. You just have to give it some time."

"And where are our parents? Why aren't they with us on this trip?"

Ginny sighed. "We're hoping to meet them along the way somewhere."

"Hoping? What do you mean, hoping? Isn't there a plan?"

"Not really," said Ginny weakly.

"Well this whole thing seems fishy to me. And I don't like how some of the people on the train seem really sick. They don't look as if they're acting. That little boy we helped yesterday even felt hot, as if he had a fever.

Ginny sighed again. It was getting harder and harder to deal with Finn's amnesia. When the man on their train had died from cholera, Finn had thought it was all an act. But as more and more people became ill, including the little boy, Benjamin, Finn was finding it hard to believe they were acting.

The whole train had stopped for a few days to deal with their invalids, but they couldn't wait much longer or they wouldn't make it over the mountains before winter set in. There was talk of leaving the sick members behind along with some volunteers to care for them. Whoever survived could catch up with the train on horseback.

* * * *

"NOOOOOO! NOOOOO!"

Finn's eyes jerked open and his heart started pounding. He had been asleep for about an hour. The sound of wailing echoed around them.

"What is it?" asked Ginny, wide-eyed.

"I don't know, but I wish those reenactors would let us get some sleep!" Finn grumbled.

Across the wagon corral, they could see lights

and people milling around the wagon where the sick boy lay.

"Oh, no!" said Ginny, "I hope Benjamin is all right."

"Let's go see," said Finn.

"Okay," said Ginny.

The twins scrambled to their feet and hastened across the corral where they could see Mrs. Campbell comforting Benjamin's mother. She looked up as Finn and Ginny approached.

"Little Benjamin has died," she told them sadly. "Could you two take his brother and sister over to your wagon to distract them for a while? It will take some time before their mother will be able to deal with them."

Tears spilled down Ginny's cheeks. "Yes, we'd be glad to help," she said.

Finn followed her to the wagon and peeked in. Little Benjamin lay still as a stone on the makeshift bed. He whispered to Ginny, "How did they get him to lie so still?"

Ginny had had enough. She turned and whispered furiously at him, "Finn, he's really dead! This isn't acting! This is real!" Finn's mouth dropped open. Ginny turned to the two little children in the corner of the wagon. "Would you two like to play with us for a while? Before we went to sleep, I saw some flowers next to our wagon. We could make a flower chain for your mother.

The two children looked at each other and

then crawled over to Ginny who helped them down from the wagon. Ginny took their hands and they made their way back to Ginny and Finn's wagon.

Finn stood motionless. Dead? Benjamin was really dead? He cautiously reached out and placed his finger on the boy's neck to check for a pulse. Then he jerked his hand away. Ginny wasn't acting. Benjamin was really dead. Finn slowly walked back to their wagon. Ginny had settled the children in their wagon and was making flower chains with them in the lantern light. Finn went to the tent, lay down, and stared up into space.

Later, Ginny joined him in the tent along with the children. No one spoke. Eventually, they all fell into an uneasy sleep.

When Ginny woke up, Finn was gone.

14

Belief

Finn shouldered his bedroll and climbed to his feet. *I'm lucky to get out of there alive,* he thought. *I don't know who those people are, but they must have kidnapped me or something. First that girl Ginny tells me we're back in time, and then she tells me they are all reenactors. I don't think reenactors would go so far as to watch their children die just to stay in character. Either that or they are really twisted people. I need to get as far away from them as possible. I'll just keep walking until I find a town and go to the police. Maybe they can help me find my family.*

Since the trail was running east to west, he decided to head straight north to avoid running into the wagon train again. He actually wanted to go south, but the Platte River was in the way.

A couple of hours later he was walking in an

area full of rolling green hills. He hadn't seen a soul since he'd left the camp. *You'd think by now I would have found a road or at least seen some power lines. I wonder where I am?*

Then he heard a rumbling sound. *Maybe there's a train nearby. I'll climb that hill to take a look.*

A few minutes later, he was standing on the top of a hill, staring in astonishment at the scene below him. The plains were covered for miles in every direction with moving buffalo. There were so many of them that he couldn't see a speck of ground between them. Stunned, he sank to the ground.

It took over an hour for the herd to pass by. As he watched, Finn did some heavy thinking. *I've made a horrible mistake. Ginny wasn't lying. I really am back in time. I don't know how or why I'm here, but this is definitely not my own time-period. There aren't that many free-roaming buffalo alive in one place in the twenty-first century. I have to get back to the wagon train as quickly as possible.*

He picked up his bedroll and started back the way he had come. *Since I traveled north, all I have to do is travel south and I'll hit the wagon trail again. I hope the train hasn't decided to leave their sick members behind and move on.*

15

Reunion

Ginny frantically searched the train for Finn, but he was nowhere to be found. Finally, she went to Captain John and told him Finn was missing.

"He still can't remember anything," she said. "I thought he was content to wait with us until he'd regained his memory, but he's confused about why he is with us. I'm not even sure he believes I'm his sister," she said wretchedly.

The captain frowned. "We were planning on leaving today, but it doesn't feel right leaving an injured boy wandering around lost on the prairie. We'll stay here one more night and spend the day sending out search parties. If we haven't found him by tomorrow morning, we're going to have to leave without him. We've already been delayed here too many days. If we don't leave soon, we'll never get over the mountains before winter sets in."

An hour later Ginny was sitting on a borrowed horse next to five men on horseback from the train. They had decided to search for Finn to the north. Another group of men had gone ahead on the trail to search for him, but Ginny thought that since Finn was trying to run from what he thought were reenactors, he would probably head away from the trail. She decided to ride with the group searching off the trail.

The searchers were not very good trackers, so they just spread out, making sure to keep within hailing distance of each other.

"Be sure to also keep an eye out for Indians," the captain warned them as they left. "If you see one, group back together immediately and be prepared to defend yourselves."

As Ginny rode along, she was almost paralyzed with fear for Finn. *What am I going to do if we can't find him? If I stay here with the sick members of the train, he might come back to this spot once he realizes he's really back in the past. But he also might go searching for the train instead. And if he doesn't realize he's really back in the past, he's in horrible danger. He doesn't know the Indians might be hostile or that there aren't any stores here to buy food, even if he had the money. He probably thinks he can just find a town and get help.* Then she squared her shoulders. *Worrying isn't going to solve this. The best way to help Finn is to find him. I need to keep looking.*

* * * *

After searching for about two hours, they decided to take a break. Ginny chewed on a piece of beef jerky as her eyes searched the empty, endless prairie.

Then she saw a spot moving toward them. "Is that a person?" she asked quickly.

The man next to her shaded his forehead and peered into the distance. "I believe it is, but I can't tell if it's a man or a boy. Let's wait until he gets a bit closer before we hail him. We don't want to take any chances. It could be an Indian scout."

They watched as the spot grew larger. Ginny's hopes grew. Was it Finn?

She jumped to her feet.

"I think it's Finn! I really think it's Finn!" She waved her arms. "Finn! Over here! Finn!"

The person in the distance stopped and looked around. When he saw them, he waved back and started running forward.

Ginny ran toward him, tears running down her cheeks. "Finn! Finn! I was so worried!"

The twins met in a huge hug. "I'm so sorry Ginny! I'm sorry I didn't believe you," Finn said.

Ginny pulled back to look at him. "Did you get your memory back?" She asked excitedly.

Finn's face fell. "No, not yet. But I do believe you that we're back in time. But how did we get here? You've never told me."

The other searchers were walking toward them.

"I'll tell you once we're back on the wagon," Ginny whispered.

One of the men gave Finn a clout on his shoulder. "You sure had us worried, son. I hope you don't ever pull such a foolish stunt again."

"I'm sorry, sir," Finn replied in a small voice. "You're right—it was foolish. Ever since I lost my memory I've been confused, but now I know I should stay with the train until my memory comes back."

16

More Deaths

That night two more of the settlers died from cholera and the remaining sick man, a bachelor named Isaac, didn't look as if he were going to survive much longer.

"I'm sorry, but we just can't continue to wait here," the captain explained to Isaac's friends. "We've delayed much too long already, and I have the welfare of the whole train to consider. You can remain here to take care of Isaac and then either catch up to us on horseback or join the next train that comes through."

Isaac's friends nodded. "It's all right, Captain," one of them said. "We understand. You need to get these good people to Oregon before winter sets in or they all might die."

"God be with you," the captain said as he signaled for the train to start moving.

That day, the dust was horrible. Ginny struggled to breath and began to choke from the dust swirling around them. Finn, who was driving the wagon, could barely see three feet in front of him.

He said to Ginny, "Why don't you drink some water and then walk ahead of the train for a while? I thought I saw Sarah walking there to keep ahead of the dust from the wagons. You could walk with her."

"Good idea," said Ginny between coughs. "This dust is terrible. I'll walk up front for a while and then come back here to give you a turn." She climbed into the back of the wagon to get the water. Finn could hear her rummaging around behind him. When she climbed back to the front of the wagon, she was holding two wet handkerchiefs. "I have an idea. If we each tie these around our nose and mouth, we can breathe through them, and that might help with the dust." She held the reins so that Finn could tie his handkerchief on.

"That was a good idea," Finn said as he slowed down the wagon so Ginny could jump off. "Thank you."

Ginny jumped down and ran alongside the train until she reached Sarah, who was walking with a group of girls.

"Isn't the dust awful?" said Sarah. "At least it's not too bad here. We just have to keep ahead of the wagons."

Ginny looked back and saw the cloud of dust

behind them. "It's so bad that I can't even see the wagons."

"There's three more!" called out one of the girls.

"Three more what?" asked Ginny.

"Three more graves," answered Sarah. "Abigail keeps a count in her journal of how many newly dug graves she sees along the trail."

Ginny grimaced. "How gruesome!"

"Actually, it's important information," said Abigail. "Someday folks might be interested in knowing how many settlers died on this trail. Besides, I think it's important to mark their passing," she said somberly. "Their families had to leave them behind. Soon their graves will disappear and no one will know they are there. I don't ever want to forget how many people died trying to settle the west."

"You're right," said Ginny thoughtfully. "It is important not to forget."

"Look, Abigail, there are seven graves across the road," said Sarah. "You'd better add them to your count."

After a while, Ginny said goodbye to the girls and headed back into the dust cloud to trade places with Finn.

That evening, Isaac's friends caught up to the train. He had died only a few hours after the train had left them.

17

The Race

"It's so dusty!" said Ginny as she cleared her throat for what felt like the hundredth time. "And with those huge droves of cattle from the other train in front of us, we can't even walk ahead of the dust today."

"I wonder if we could get ahead of them?" mused Finn.

They were second in line today behind the captain's wagon, but ahead of them were about fifty wagons and several hundred head of cattle from another train. The dust was so bad that they could barely see the captain's wagon in front of them.

Finn peered through the dust and saw the captain start to pull his wagon toward the left side of the road in an attempt to pass the other train.

Then he heard one of the cattlemen in front of him yell angrily, "We don't want to ride behind your dust! If you try to pass us, we'll drive our cattle all over you!"

Captain John ignored him and kept on going. Finn started to pull his wagon to follow when he heard Ginny gasp. He looked ahead and saw that some of the cattlemen had pulled out their pistols. Even worse, one of them had galloped over to the captain and pointed it at his head. "I said, don't try to pass us!" he shouted.

Just then, Mr. Knight, who was driving the wagon behind Finn, pulled his wagon completely off the road and shouted, "Boys, follow me!"

Finn quickly followed him out into the open country. Ginny peered behind and saw the other wagons in their train following, including Captain John who had managed to get away from the angry cattleman.

When the head teamster of the other train saw what was happening, he tried to whip his cattle into going faster, but it was no use. Their train was just too large. Soon they were out of sight and Captain John pulled his team back onto the road.

"What a bunch of jerks!" said Ginny once everything had calmed down. "I can't believe that man was actually going to shoot Captain John over something so silly."

"I wonder if he really would have shot him?" asked Finn.

"Well, he shouldn't have pulled a weapon unless he meant to use it," said Ginny.

Not too long after that, they saw a good grazing spot for their cattle, so the captain called for a break. Finn and Ginny had just sat down to eat some bread and cheese when Ginny spotted the other wagon train in the distance.

"Oh no! They're catching up to us!" she cried.

Captain John saw the train at the same time.

"Quick, everyone! Back to the wagons! We worked too hard to get ahead of them to lose our place now!"

Pans clattered and boxes banged as everyone rushed to put their supplies back in the wagons. Finn and Ginny pulled themselves up onto the wagon and soon were ready to go. They moved into line and stayed ahead of the cattlemen for the rest of the trip.

18

Pandemonium

"**L**ook at that beautiful table! I can't believe that someone threw it out!" exclaimed Sarah. The girls were stretching their legs by walking alongside the wagon train.

"I wish we could pick it up and take it with us to Oregon," said Abigail. "But I'm sure we don't have room in our wagon."

"Plus, it must be awfully heavy," said Ginny. "That's most likely why the owners threw it out. Their oxen were probably getting tired from hauling it so far."

"Let's try to list everything we've seen dumped on the road," suggested Abigail. "I bet we could furnish a whole house with what folks have dumped on the side of road!"

"I saw a bedstead, a cook stove, and lots of blankets and quilts," said Ginny.

"And I saw a cupboard, a feather bed, chairs, and some books," added Sarah. "I also saw a big pile of stuff with a sign on it that said 'Help yourself.'"

"Did any of you notice the abandoned wagon about a mile back?" asked Abigail. "Why would someone abandon a wagon?"

"Perhaps their oxen died," suggested Ginny.

"Or maybe their driver died of cholera," said Sarah somberly.

The other girls were quiet.

Without warning, a scream cut through the silence. Ginny quickly turned her head as more and more screams could be heard.

Behind them was pandemonium. A man on horseback raced past them. He was covered with bells that made a huge racket and scared the teams. The frightened oxen and horses raced in all directions, scattering screaming women and children as they went.

A wide-eyed team of oxen bore down on the girls. The frantic driver yelled, "Get out of the way! Get out of the way!"

Ginny and the other girls jumped to the side of the road. There was a rush of wind as the runaway team went wildly on down the road. The girls ran until they were safely away from the frantic animals. Then they turned and stared back at the scene behind them. Wagons were overturned. A man, his face white with pain, held his arm. Children cried. And in the distance, they saw some teams still fleeing wildly away.

"What was that man thinking, riding by us with bells like that?" exclaimed Ginny angrily. "Just last week that woman on the train ahead of us died from being run over during a wagon train stampede!"

"I hope he doesn't reach their train," said Sarah. "They've had enough grief with stampedes. That woman and her baby died and two other men were crippled when their train stampeded."

"I hope no one was hurt in our stampede!" cried Abigail.

The girls looked worriedly at each other and then rushed back toward the scattered train. Ginny searched frantically for Finn. She finally found him and their overturned wagon about a mile from the road. He'd already unhitched the oxen, which were off to the side placidly chewing on some grass.

"Are you all right?" Ginny asked.

"Yes, no thanks to that crazy man," said Finn. "I managed to jump from the wagon before it overturned, so I only have some bruises. But our wagon broke its hind axle."

"Oh, no! Can we fix it?" said Ginny.

Finn shook his head wearily. "I don't know. Could you go back and find Mr. Campbell to tell him what's happened? I think I should stay here with the oxen to make sure they don't take fright again."

Ginny brought Mr. Campbell back to look at

the broken wagon. He shook his head in dismay.

"I don't know where we're going to get another axle to fix this. We're out in the middle of no-where."

Ginny's face brightened. "What about using that abandoned wagon we saw a couple of miles back? Would the axle from that fit?"

Mr. Campbell's face cleared. "You know, that just might work. What a great idea, Ginny! We'll take my team back to the other wagon and use it to haul it back here for parts. There might be other folks who need pieces from it, too."

The hind axle from the abandoned wagon fit perfectly

19

Desert

"Be sure to fill all of your water casks," the captain warned. "Tomorrow we're leaving the Platte River and heading toward the Sweetwater River. Ahead of us are fifty miles with almost no fresh water. And whatever you do, don't let your oxen drink any standing water that you see. It will most likely be poisonous!"

When the captain was finished speaking, the crowd of pioneers who had been standing around him turned away and headed back to their wagons. Finn looked over at Ginny. Her face was swollen from gnat bites.

"Well, at least we're finally away from those awful buffalo gnats," he said.

"I don't know how much more of them I could stand! They swarmed so much that I had to scrape them off the hot pan before I could cook the bacon yesterday! I'd heard of them literally driving animals crazy, but I never realized how bad they could really be."

"Everyone on the train has so many bites that we all look as if we have smallpox," Finn said.

"Well I'm glad that we're finally away from them. We'd better start filling water casks. We have a desert to travel through tomorrow."

* * * *

The next afternoon Ginny looked around at the sagebrush-covered land. There was very little grass for the oxen to eat. The wagon rode through a dried-up pond crusted with what looked like dried soda or salt. The oxen's hoofs crunched through the crust as they walked. She wrinkled her nose as they drove by a dead ox covered with flies.

Suddenly there was a commotion in the front of the wagon train. Ginny and Finn craned their necks to see what was happening.

"It looks as if someone's oxen drank water from that pond in front of us," commented Finn.

"Oh no!" exclaimed Ginny. "The captain warned us about that. The ponds are poisonous!"

"Didn't the driver see all of the dead animals along the side of the road? I'm sure they died from drinking the water," said Finn.

As they drove by the wagon that had pulled to

the side of the road, Finn asked, "What happened? Do you need any help?"

"I fell asleep while I was driving, and before I knew what was going on, the oxen had started drinking from the pond," the man said ruefully. "Luckily, the team tied to the back of the wagon wasn't able to reach the water." He looked sorrowfully at the oxen that had drunk the water. They were already staggering around looking ill. "I'll have to leave them here and use my other team to pull the wagon. You kids go ahead. I can handle this."

"Poor man," said Ginny as they went on their way.

"At least he has a spare team to pull his wagon. We'll have to be extra careful that we don't fall asleep on this part of the trail," said Finn.

"It's hard not to sometimes. Driving a wagon can be really boring."

* * * *

A few hours later, Finn pulled on the reins. "Looks like a traffic jam. I wonder what's going on?"

"I'll run ahead and see why we've stopped," said Ginny as she hopped off the wagon. She ran forward and found the captain talking to a group of pioneers from their train.

"This is the only fresh, clean water for miles," the captain said. "But it is an extremely slow spring, and you can only gather a cupful of water at a time."

Ginny looked around her. There were over a hundred people and their wagons patiently waiting for their turn at the springs.

"It's going to take us all afternoon to water our teams!" exclaimed one of the men.

"We'll camp here and rest while we're waiting," said the captain. "Then, once we've watered the teams, we'll head out immediately, even if it's dark. It will be a little more dangerous traveling at night, but it will be cooler. With luck, we should reach fresh water tomorrow."

20

Water!

"**W**hoa! Whoa!" shouted Finn as the oxen raced toward the river. He pulled frantically on the reins, stopping them just at the edge of the bank. They dipped their head in the water and started drinking.

Ginny wiped her brow. "That was a close call. They almost ran right into the water!"

"Driving through a desert sure makes you thirsty," said Finn as he jumped off the wagon. "I almost feel like jumping in myself."

"Look out! Get out of the way!" yelled another driver as his wagon come racing toward them. The driver pulled hard on the reins, but his oxen wouldn't stop. They plunged right into the water, tipping the wagon over as they went. As it turned upside down, a woman screamed.

Ginny gasped. "She's inside the wagon!"

The driver jumped off and yelled, "Help me get them out of here!"

Finn and Ginny rushed to help. The wagon was completely upside down. Finn grabbed his knife and held his breath as he dove under the water, frantically slicing through the wagon cover to get to the woman trapped inside. The driver dove in next to him and helped him rip the cover open and drag the struggling woman to the surface. As they came up for air, Finn could see that she was clinging to a small boy who immediately started to howl.

"Is there anyone else in there?" Ginny asked over his cries.

"No, no one else," the woman gasped. "Thank you so much for rescuing us."

More people came over to help and the wagon was soon turned upright again.

* * * *

The next morning Ginny was driving the team along the Sweetwater River when she nudged Finn, who had fallen asleep next to her. "Finn, wake up! Look over there!"

Finn raised his head and rubbed his eyes. "What is it?"

"It's Independence Rock! I remember it from our history book!"

Finn looked off to the right and saw a mound

of rock rising out of the dry ground. At that moment, the wagon train stopped. "What's going on?" he wondered out loud.

"I bet we're stopping so that folks can hike to the rock," said Ginny. "It's famous. People traveling on the Oregon Trail would stop and carve their names in it."

Ginny pulled the wagon to a stop. The twins jumped down and walked over to where the captain was standing. He was beaming.

"What's happening?" asked Ginny.

"We've reached Independence Rock before the Fourth of July! Rumor has it that we need to be here by the fourth to make it over the mountains before winter sets in."

"Do you think the rumor is true?" asked Finn.

The captain grinned. "Let's hope so," he said. "But we're not going to slow down just because we're here before the fourth. We'll stop here for a short time so that folks can hike to the rock. But not too long. We have a mountain to get over before winter!"

Finn and Ginny joined the group of pioneers who walked to the rock. Ginny placed her hand on its warm surface and watched the others as they painted their names on the rock.

One of the women turned to the twins after she had finished writing her name. "Would you like to use the rest of our paint and put your names on Independence Rock? We made it from gunpowder and bacon grease."

"Yes, please!" said Ginny excitedly. The woman handed Ginny the pot of grease and turned to walk back to the train.

Ginny whispered to Finn, "Let's put our names on the rock! Then, when we go home, we can come here in the future and find them!"

"Good idea!" said Finn.

They carefully painted their names on the rock then slowly walked back to the wagon.

Well, we haven't found Mom and Dad on this trip, but we've sure had some fun adventures," said Ginny.

"I just wish that I could *remember* Mom and Dad," Finn said quietly.

21

Traders

Finn sighed and slumped in his seat as he held the reins.

"What's wrong?" asked Ginny.

"I wish I could remember *something*, anything about my life. My only memories are of this wagon train."

Ginny chewed on her lip. "Well, I wish we could take you to a modern doctor. Then maybe we could find out when you will get your memory back."

"If I ever get it back," said Finn glumly.

"Of course you will!" Ginny said stoutly. "It just takes time for these things to heal. You could get it back any day now."

Finn glanced up. "Look ahead! Something is happening! It's like a city of tents. There must be hundreds of them!"

Just then the train slowed to a stop. "I wonder what it is?" mused Ginny.

Ginny's friend, Sarah, walked over to their wagon. "Do you know why we're stopped?" she asked.

"I don't know," said Finn. "Why don't you two walk ahead and see what's happening."

Ginny hopped off the wagon and walked along with Sarah. As they got closer to the front of the train, they could see a group of angry people gathered around the captain.

"It's outrageous! They can't do this to us!" yelled one man.

"We can't pay that!" yelled another.

Ginny and Sarah walked over to a woman standing off to the side with tears streaming down her face.

"What's wrong?" asked Ginny.

"The traders have taken over the ferry and are charging eighteen dollars per wagon to cross," she sadly explained.

"Eighteen dollars!" exclaimed Sarah. "That's a fortune!"

"We don't have eighteen dollars," the woman sobbed. "We'll have to turn back."

"Why can't we just go across ourselves?" asked Ginny. "Why do we need their ferries?"

"The traders say that they've made a deal with the local Indians and that the Indians will attack us if we don't use their boats," the woman said.

Just then, the girls heard Captain John's voice. "Calm down, everyone! Calm down! Let's stop for the day, and I'll meet with the other train captains to see what we can do about this. In the meantime, fill your water casks and get some rest. We'll have a meeting later to discuss the situation."

The next morning a general meeting of all the wagon trains was called. One of the pioneers stood up on a box and called out to the group. "Everyone, we need to be careful. We don't want to do anything that will set the Indians on us. I suggest that we try to compromise with the traders. Maybe we can get them to lower their prices."

"Our train has been sitting here for a week!" yelled a man from one of the other wagon trains. "Don't you understand? They won't compromise! I'm done trying to compromise!"

"Me, too!" shouted another man. "And me!" piped up a woman's voice. All around people muttered in agreement as the first man climbed down from the box shaking his head.

Another man jumped onto the box. "Folks, we have a choice. We can either sit here and wait, losing valuable time, or we can do something about these ferries. I suggest we do something! Today is the Fourth of July! Our ancestors didn't fight and die for our freedom so we could be told by a bunch of traders that we can't cross a river! Everyone who agrees with me raise their hands!"

Finn and Ginny watched as all around them hands rose into the air. Cheers erupted throughout the crowd. Cries of "Let's cross the river!" grew louder and louder until almost everyone was chanting, "Let's cross the river!"

A couple of hours later, Finn and Ginny watched a group of men from the different wagon trains shoulder their rifles and march toward the ferry boats. They surrounded the traders. One of the traders shouted, "You can't do this! These are our boats!"

"Don't worry, we'll pay you for their use," said the captain, "but it will be a *fair* price."

Suddenly, on the other side of the bank, a group of Indians appeared from behind some rocks. They milled around shouting war-whoops and then they quickly mounted their horses and rode off.

"You're going to be sorry now!" yelled one of the traders. "They're going off to get the rest of the tribe to slaughter you."

Captain John spoke up. "Then you'd better pray that doesn't happen. Because if any Indian or trader fires a shot at us, you folks will be the first to die."

While one group of men kept guard on the traders, other men started running the ferry boats. As the wagons landed on the far side of the river, they were parked so they formed a half-circle corral with the river on the open end. Once all of the various wagon trains were across, the loose stock was swum over into the wagon corral.

A third group of men had kept count of every wagon that went over. When all the wagons were across, the angry traders were paid four dollars for each wagon that had crossed the river.

"You're going to regret this!" one of the traders shouted. "The Indians are going to wipe out each and every one of you!"

A woman began to cry. "Why didn't we pay? Aren't our lives worth a few more dollars?"

A man standing next to her said, "Madam, it's not only the money. It's the principle of it. Those men had no right to take over the river. This is a free country and no one can tell us whether we can or can't cross a river. They wouldn't even let us make our own boats and cross. We couldn't let them get away with that. If you start letting people take away your freedoms, there's no telling when it will stop. Then all of a sudden you wake up one day to find that you're not living in a free country anymore."

* * * *

That night a guard was kept on the traders. All the men kept their rifles handy and sentries were posted. The night passed quietly.

The next morning, the captains of the various wagon trains decided that all the trains should ride together for a few days in case the Indians attacked. Ginny drove the wagon as it fell into line in the middle of the long train of wagons. Two hundred men rode on either side of the wagons, guarding them from attack. There were more men riding ahead to watch for Indians. The Indians never attacked, and a few days later the long train broke up and each wagon train went on its way.

22

Soda Springs

"Ginny, wake up!" Finn shook his sister with one arm while holding the reins with the other.

Ginny sat up and rubbed her eyes. On the right side of the road there was a mound of earth five feet high with water bubbling out over the top.

"What is it?" she asked.

"I heard the captain talking about this area last night," Finn replied. "This whole place is full of natural springs that taste like soda water. He said that it's a favorite camping spot, so we're going to stop here for the night. There is also a warm spring where we can wash clothes."

The tired travelers gratefully stopped for the rest of the day and enjoyed the springs. Ginny and Finn were washing their clothes in one of the warm springs when Mrs. Campbell came over to them with a cup of water. "Would you like to try some sweetened soda water?" she asked. "I've added a little tartaric acid and sugar to it and it's quite good."

"Thank you," said Ginny as she took a taste from the cup. Her eyes widened, "Finn, it tastes like soda pop!"

"Good, isn't it?" said Mrs. Campbell. "I've also used it to bake biscuits for dinner tonight. They came out wonderfully light and fluffy. The water here is truly special."

That night another train camped near them and there was an impromptu party. Some of the men pulled out their fiddles and Ginny and Finn joined in the dancing. The next morning, everyone was tired, but more relaxed and happy than they had been in a while.

But then the captain made an announcement. "I spoke with the captain from the other train last night. They tried to cross the Snake River, but the crossing is too deep and swift right now. They turned back and are going to take the trail that runs south of the river. Luckily for us, they decided to stop at Soda Springs one more time before they headed west, or we would have run into the same problem. I'd been hoping we could take the north trail because it has more grass and water, but it looks as if we'll have to take the dryer, south trail. Everyone needs to fill their water casks and prepare for a long, dry journey."

23

Difficulties

Finn, Ginny, and Mr. Campbell looked down sorrowfully on the dead ox. "Why do you think he died?" Ginny sobbed.

"I don't know for sure," replied Mr. Campbell, "but he's not the only one. More oxen are dying every day. I'm glad I brought some extra teams, but at this rate we may have to use the cows to pull the wagons like some of the other pioneers." He stood silently for a moment looking down at his dead ox. "I think we should lighten our loads. Perhaps the oxen are just getting worn out with all of the work they've been doing. Next time we stop, we'll go through the wagons and toss out everything that is not absolutely necessary."

Mr. Campbell wasn't the only one to decide to lighten his loads. For the rest of the day, Ginny and Finn saw piles of goods along the side of the road, many of them with signs on them that said, "Help Yourselves!"

That evening, when they pulled into their campsite, Ginny wrinkled her nose. "Ewww! What's that awful stench?" she asked. "It smells as if something died here!"

"Something did die here," said Finn as he pointed to a pile of carcasses. "Oxen. It seems as if every campsite has more and more dead ones."

The twins helped the Campbells sort through their gear to lighten their wagons' loads. Mrs. Campbell handed Ginny some extra bedding to toss on the discard pile. "Have you noticed how gloomy everyone is?" she asked. "We were all so happy not that long ago at Soda Springs, but now no one seems to smile or laugh anymore."

"It's been a long journey," observed Ginny. "And it seems as if it's getting harder, not easier. I think the people are getting as worn out as the oxen."

"And folks are worried about the mountains in front of us. We've heard so many horrible stories about how hard they are to cross." Mrs. Campbell sighed. "It feels as if we may never reach the settlements on the other side."

* * * *

Early the next morning, Finn heard a man's voice yelling, "He stole my horse! That Indian stole my horse!" A group of men quickly formed around the stricken man, Mr. Strong.

"Look out there!" Mr. Strong pointed. "You can see him riding in the distance."

Finn looked where the man was pointing and could barely see the dust cloud where the Indian was riding off.

"Quick! If we hurry, we can catch him!" yelled Mr. Strong as he rushed to mount another horse. Three other men jumped on their horses to join him, and soon they were riding after the fleeing Indian.

A couple of hours later, one of the men, Mr. Godfrey, came galloping back. "Hadley's been shot! Someone get the doctor!"

Ginny turned worriedly to Finn, "It's a good thing Doctor Cole joined our train awhile back. I hope Mr. Hadley is all right."

The twins watched as Mr. Godfrey led the doctor and six others out of the camp to fetch the wounded man. That night as they sat around the campfire, they heard the story of what happened.

"We caught up with the Indian about twelve miles outside of camp," said Mr. Godfrey. "He had hidden himself on a ledge of rocks and when we rode close to him, he shot Hadley. The ball passed between Hadley's ribs and went right through him, but it doesn't appear to have hit anything vital. The doctor says he has a chance of surviving if we keep him quiet and give him time to heal."

They spent the next two days in camp, giving

Mr. Hadley time to recover. The men were put on extra watches to keep an eye out for more Indians. On the third day, the wagon train started on its way again.

24

The Voice

Finn was walking with his friend Jim when Jim's dad, the captain, rode over to them. "Would you boys like to help scout the trail with me? I want to find a place for us to camp tonight."

"Sure, Dad! That would be great!" exclaimed Jim. "Do you want to go, Finn?"

"Yes, but I don't have a horse," Finn said.

"That's no problem, son. You can borrow one of our horses," said the captain.

"Let me go tell Ginny where I'm going," said Finn. He ran back and then quickly returned.

Jim's mother slowed their wagon down so Finn and Jim could unhook the horses that were hitched to the back. Soon they were riding ahead of the wagon train with Jim's dad.

About a half an hour after the train was out of sight, they came to a fork in the road in front of a large lake. One branch of the fork went around one side of the lake and the other branch went around the other side.

"Let's try the trail that looks more traveled on," said the captain as he turned his horse in that direction.

Finn was just thinking how much he enjoyed being away from the dust and noise of the wagon train when all of a sudden a voice rang out, "Turn back!"

Finn glanced around and asked Jim, "Did you say something?"

Jim looked bewildered. "No, it wasn't me. Did you hear it, Dad?"

The captain frowned. "Yes, I heard it." He looked around uneasily. There was no one in sight and no trees or brush nearby for anyone to hide behind. "Let's keep riding, but keep your eyes open for danger," he said.

Finn nervously looked all around as they went on down the trail. Suddenly, the voice rang out again, "Turn back!"

The captain stopped for a moment, and then kept riding on. Finn and Jim followed.

Then, they heard the voice a third time. "Turn back!" They looked around, and, again, there was no place for anyone to hide.

The captain stopped. "That does it. We're going back," he said. "I'm not going to ignore three warnings." He turned his horse around and the two boys followed. When they reached the fork, they left rocks as a marker to guide the wagon train onto the less-used trail and rode along it until they found a nice campsite.

Soon after the wagon train had arrived and they had set up camp, a company of soldiers arrived. Finn was on his way to get some water from the lake when the officer in charge stopped him.

"Son, can you bring me to the captain of this train?"

"Yes, sir," Finn replied. "He's over by those trees. I'll bring you to him."

The officer dismounted from his horse and followed Finn over to the captain.

After shaking Captain John's hand, the officer said, "My name is Officer Jenkins and we're out on the road to protect the pioneers," he said. "Have you seen any Indians around?"

"No, but we had a strange experience earlier," replied the captain. "We were on the branch of the trail on the other side of the lake when we kept hearing a voice telling us to turn back. We heard it three different times and each time we heard it there was no one in sight."

The officer's eyes widened. "That was a warning, and you did well to heed it. The train ahead of you was ambushed by Indians when they were camped on that trail. Many folks were killed— very few escaped!"

Finn and Captain John stared at each other in shock.

"And to think we almost kept going," whispered the captain. "We were truly saved by a miracle."

25

Mountains

"I can't believe we were so anxious to get here," complained Ginny. "I think riding up and down these mountains is the worst part of the trail."

"I don't know about that," said Finn. "Worse than the cholera? Or the Indian attacks? Or the flood?"

"It's just so scary on these steep trails," said Ginny. "Especially when we're going downhill— like the trail we're about to go on now." She looked over to the wagon ahead of them as a group of men prepared to take it down the steep hill. The wheels had chains on them that locked them to the frame of the wagon and kept them from turning. Mr. Campbell and another man were stationed on either side of the oxen to make sure they didn't stray off the narrow path and fall into the river far below.

The twins watched tensely as the wagon inched its way down the mountain. Then, just as it reached the bottom, it started sliding out of control. The oxen bellowed as the wagon flipped over onto its side, striking Mr. Campbell and knocking him to the side as it rolled.

"Oh, no!" cried Ginny. "Mr. Campbell is hurt!" The twins scrambled down the steep slope as fast as they could to help him.

"Are you all right?" asked Finn as they reached the fallen man.

Mr. Campbell looked up ruefully at them. "I'll be fine," he said. "I'm just a bit bruised. I'm much luckier than the man yesterday who was killed when his wagon fell on him."

Finn and Ginny helped Mr. Campbell to his feet. "I think we'll try tying a rope to the end of the next wagon and lower it down," he suggested as he brushed himself off. "That might give us better control of it."

* * * *

Later that night, after all the wagons had been brought down the hill without any more incidents, Ginny turned to Finn.

"Do you know we only have forty-five days left in this time period? We'll be going home in a month and a half."

"And I still can't remember anything before

this wagon ride," said Finn miserably. "I'm beginning to wonder if I will ever remember anything from my past."

"I know you will!" said Ginny. "You'll get better. You just have to be patient."

"I can't even remember Mom and Dad!" said Finn. "How can I help look for them if I don't even know what they look like?"

"I can always show you pictures when we get home," said Ginny. "But I bet I won't need to. I think when we get home and you start seeing familiar things, you'll start remembering again."

"I sure hope you're right," said Finn.

26

The Dalles

Ginny stared in astonishment at the crowd of people. Their train had just come off the trail at the Dalles, a place on the Columbia River where many pioneers loaded onto boats and went downstream. They were surrounded by the motliest group of people she'd ever seen.

Some were dressed in rags, some were in their best clothes, and some had almost no clothes at all. One woman was wearing what looked like her Sunday best dress, but she had no shoes. Another woman had shoes, but her dress had so many patches on it that you couldn't see the original material. There were half-naked children running in all directions. The one thing everyone wore in common was dust. There was dust everywhere, and they were all coated with it.

But, in spite of the crowds and the dust, there

were some happy faces. The worst part of the trail was over. From here, many of the pioneers would be going downstream to their final destination, the Willamette Valley.

The captain gathered the people from their wagon train together for a final meeting.

"Folks, this is where our wagon train ends. There are boats for hire here to take you down the river. However, there are some falls you will have to ride around. You will need to take your wagons apart to get them on the boats that will take you to the falls. Your oxen will have to go by pack trail. Once you are at the falls, you will unload your belongings, put your wagons together and, when your oxen arrive, you will ride your wagons around the falls. Then you will take everything apart again to load it back onto a boat that will take you to the mouth of the Sandy River in the Willamette Valley."

When the captain finished speaking, everyone got busy preparing for the next part of their journey.

Mr. Campbell came over to the twins. "I'm going to take our oxen over the pack trail myself. I would like it if you two could go with Mrs. Campbell and the baby on the boat. I'd be much obliged if you would watch out for her. She's not been feeling well lately."

"Of course," said Ginny. "We'll take care of her for you."

The next day was spent unloading the wagons

and taking them apart. When that was finished, Mr. Campbell went on his way with the oxen while the twins sat down with Mrs. Campbell and the baby to wait for their turn on a boat. Finn and Ginny watched the boats being loaded. First the wagon gears were loaded on, then the wagon boxes. Everything else was piled on top of the boxes.

"Where are we going to fit?" asked Ginny.

Finn pointed. "I guess we'll be sitting on top of everything, like those folks over there."

The next morning, it was their turn. Finn and Ginny helped Mrs. Campbell and the baby on board. They spread a feather bed out for her to lie on and then sat down next to her.

"We're packed in here like sardines," said Finn as the boat took off.

When they reached midstream, Ginny frowned. "Doesn't this boat seem a bit low in the water?" she asked.

Finn watched as a wave sloshed over the side. "Yes, it does! I think they've overloaded it!"

Another wave sloshed over and a woman cried out, "We're going to sink!"

Immediately people started to panic. Cries of "We're going to sink! We're going to sink!" echoed everywhere.

"Don't worry, folks!" shouted the captain. "We're just a bit overloaded. I'm going to land and some of you can get off and wait for the next boat."

A little further downstream was a narrow sandy beach with a cliff behind it. The captain pulled the boat onto the beach and pointed at about fifteen people, including Finn, Ginny, and Mrs. Campbell. "You folks get off here and we'll come back for you as soon as we can. Be sure to grab your tents and supplies."

Finn and Ginny helped Mrs. Campbell off the boat and unloaded all of their gear. Then they stood on the sandy beach and watched the boat head downstream.

27

Death on the River

Ginny morosely watched another boat pass by. It had been seven days since the boat captain had dropped them on the sandy beach, and still no one had stopped to pick them up. They had started to run out of provisions, so Finn and some of the men had hiked five miles back to the Dalles to buy some of the expensive food that was available for sale there. Ginny had stayed back to care for Mrs. Campbell and the baby. She turned to Mrs. Campbell and said, "I'm so glad you are feeling better today."

Mrs. Campbell smiled. "I am too, though I am worried about that poor boy, Clark Anderson. I don't think he's going to make it."

"I feel awful for his parents. I heard they didn't want him to come to Oregon, but he left without their permission. Now he's out here sick with no family to take care of him."

Finn and the men soon arrived back at camp. Finn sat down next to Ginny.

"There wasn't much food available," he said. "Though I managed to buy some tea and crackers. However, there is some good news. The boat is going to pick us up tomorrow!"

"That's great!" said Ginny. "I'm getting really tired of this beach."

* * * *

The next afternoon they again found themselves perched on top of a pile of goods, going down the river. Ginny closed her eyes and felt the breeze on her face.

"It feels so good to be finally moving," she said. Then she looked at Finn. "Why do you look so worried?" she asked.

"The wind is getting stronger, and we're pretty heavily loaded."

"Not again!" said Ginny. "You don't think we're going to have to land again because we're overloaded, do you?" Tears filled her eyes.

Finn nodded glumly. "Yes, I think that's exactly what is happening. The captain is heading toward that flat spot on the opposite shore."

Once the boat had landed, the captain announced, "Folks, we're only going to stay here until the wind dies down, so don't unload everything. We'll sleep on the boat tonight and hope the wind is better in the morning."

The next morning, they started off again, but their trip was soon interrupted by a woman's sobs.

"He's died, poor Clark Anderson has died," she cried.

The captain went over to her and looked down at the dead child. "Poor boy," he said. "We'll stop here and bury him.

Later, as they stood quietly at Clark Anderson's grave, Finn reflected on how many people had died traveling west to find a new life.[d]

---

[d] It has been estimated that one out of every seventeen people died on the trail.

28

Falls

W e're here!" Ginny cried. "We've made it to the falls!" Then her eyes widened. "Look at all the people."

"How do they all fit there?" Finn wondered aloud. They looked at the narrow strip of bank crowded with people.

"Half of them look sick," commented Ginny. "I think we should leave here as soon as possible."

Mrs. Campbell came over to them and scanned the shore. "I don't see my husband. We're going to have to wait until he arrives with the oxen before we can move on."

They reluctantly unloaded and found a place to camp on the crowded shore. It was a tight fit. A few days later, Mr. Campbell finally arrived. They hurriedly put the wagons back together and loaded them so they could ride around the falls.

"I can't wait to get out of here," whispered Finn to Ginny as they started down the trail. "I feel as if we're in a germ factory."

"I know. This place is full of sick people," she said. "I'm amazed we haven't caught anything."

"Well, we've been careful to boil our water before we drink it and we've been washing our hands a lot, so that must have helped."

They soon finished the five-mile ride. As Ginny climbed down from the wagon, she said quietly, "Finn, this was our last wagon ride. The time machine will be sending us home in a few days."

Finn patted the wagon as he jumped down. "It's been an interesting adventure. I just wish I hadn't lost my memory."

"You'll get it back," Ginny assured him. "I know you will!" She looked around. "It doesn't seem as crowded here as at the last landing spot. I wonder how long we'll have to wait for another boat?"

Mr. Campbell came over to them. "I'll be taking the cattle down the pack trail in the morning. I'd appreciate it if you would watch out for Mrs. Campbell and the baby again on the next boat. She tells me that your care of her when she was sick might have saved her life. I can't thank you enough for helping her. We're in your debt."

Ginny smiled. "That's what friends are for, sir. We were happy to help out."

A week later, the boat arrived to take them on the final leg of their journey.

29

The Boat

Once again the twins found themselves perched on top of a pile of goods traveling down the river. There were about sixty people in this boat, mostly women and children since many of the men were taking the cattle and horses downstream by pack trail. A number of the people on the boat looked sick, and they all looked worn and thin.

Ginny glanced over at the family next to them, a young couple and the husband's sister. She whispered to Finn, "That man looks very ill. I don't think he's going to survive the journey. His wife and sister look so sad."

Just then the two women began to sing softly to the sick man,

> *"Mid Pleasures and palaces though I may roam,*
> *Be it ever so humble, there's no place like home;*
> *A charm from the sky seems to hallow us there,*
> *Which, seek thro' the world, is ne'er met elsewhere."*

As they reached the chorus, other people on the boat started softly singing along with them,

> *"Home! Home! Sweet, sweet home!*
> *There's no place like home.*
> *There's no place like home!"*

They floated under the shadow of a mountain as they started into the second verse,

> *"An exile from home, splendor dazzles in vain,*
> *Oh, give me my lowly thatched cottage again."*

At that moment the meaning of the words seemed to hit everyone at the same time and sobbing started breaking out all over the boat. As the sounds of grief grew louder, Ginny looked over at the boatmen with tears in her eyes and saw that they had pulled up their oars and had tears streaming down their faces. Thoughts of the hardships and losses of the journey had descended on the whole boat at once.

And then, suddenly, someone started laughing. First one person, then two, then everyone on the boat was laughing hysterically. Soon all of the previous grief was washed away. They had made it. They had survived the journey.

30

Journey's End

Ginny turned to Finn as she looked out over the crowd of people at the boat's final landing site.

"We have to make sure that we stick together. Today is the day the time machine sends us home. Since I have the time remote, you need to stay next to me in this crowd or you might get trapped back in time like Mom and Dad."

Finn nodded as he followed Ginny off the boat. They had already said their goodbyes to Mrs. Campbell, who was staying with friends until her husband arrived with the oxen.

"Let's find a quiet place where we can sit until the time machine sends us home," he said. "What does moving through time feel like? I can't remember anything about it."

"It feels—"

Ginny came to an abrupt halt and stared into the crowd.

"Mommy! Daddy!" she screamed as she tore away from Finn.

At that moment Finn started feeling nauseated. He grabbed his stomach. *I remember! This is what it feels like right before we move through time! I have to grab hold of Ginny before it's too late!*

He scanned the crowd and saw her about twenty feet in front of him trying to push her way through the mass of people. He started shoving people aside as he desperately tried to reach her.

"Ginny! Wait for me!" he yelled, but she didn't hear him.

"Ginny, wait!" He had almost reached her when the crowd parted and he saw his parents. Time stood still. All of his past came rushing back and he could remember everything again. Then, another wave of nausea hit him and he reached out and grabbed Ginny's arm.

"Let go of me!" Ginny said angrily, trying to jerk away. Then she yelled, "Mommy! Daddy! I'm over here!"

Their mother looked up. Her eyes grew wide and she yelled, "Finn! Ginny!"

Their father's head jerked around. Just as his eyes met Finn's the world started spinning and Finn felt the pull of the time machine.

Finn quickly yelled, "The Bains at Camp

Creek, Nebraska! We'll meet you at the Bains' house at Camp Creek, Nebraska!"

His father's face broke out into a huge smile. "We'll meet you there!" he yelled.

And then everything went black.

* * * *

The twins tumbled to the floor in their living room.

Immediately, Ginny rolled herself into a little ball, her back to Finn. "Why did you grab me?" she sobbed. "I could have reached them!"

Finn put his hand on her back. "No, you couldn't have. The time machine was taking us back. There was no way you could have reached them in time. And if we'd gotten separated, you would have come back here by yourself. Then you would have lost all of us."

Ginny snuffled and then was silent for a while. "I guess you're right," she said reluctantly. "And at least now we have a place to try to meet them. Why did you say we'd meet them at Camp Creek?" She stopped and stared. "And how did you remember that?" she said excitedly. "Did your memory come back?"

Finn grinned. "Yes, it did! When I saw Mom and Dad everything came back to me. I'm not sure why I thought of Uncle Alexander and Camp Creek, but it's a good idea. It took us a whole time-traveling trip to get to Oregon. If

Mom and Dad stayed there to meet us, we could spend our whole next trip trying to get there and never quite make it."

Ginny nodded but then sighed sadly. "That makes sense. Still, I wish we'd had just a few more minutes. If we'd had, Mom and Dad would be with us right now."

"Don't think about that," urged Finn. "Think about how now we know where to meet them! We've actually seen them! We're finally going to rescue them!"

"Let's go back right away!" said Ginny.

"I'm not sure about that," said Finn. "I have no idea how time moves in both places. If we go back too soon, they may not have had time to get to Camp Creek."

"Well, then, let's go tomorrow," said Ginny.

"Okay, let's go tomorrow."

Historical Notes

A lot happened in the United States and the world between Finn and Ginny's Revolutionary War adventure and their pioneer adventure. The Revolutionary War in the United States helped inspire the French Revolution which started in 1789. Then, in 1799, Napoleon came to power and started his conquest of continental Europe. His war in Europe had profound effects across the ocean in the United States.

Due to their war with Napoleon, the British starting imposing trade restrictions that upset the United States. They also started capturing United States sailors and forcing them to fight in the British Navy. Eventually, due to these and other reasons, the United States declared war on Britain—the War of 1812.

The War of 1812 ended in 1814, as did the Napoleonic Wars. But one of the biggest consequences for the United States of the Napoleonic Wars happened when Napoleon sold the Louisiana Territory to the United States in 1803 to help fund his wars. Thomas Jefferson was president at the time and it may have been the most significant act of his presidency. The Louisiana Purchase doubled the size of the United States and opened the way for the pioneers. In 1804 President Jefferson sent Meriwether Lewis and

William Clark on an expedition to explore the new territory and find a route to the west. This became known as the Lewis and Clark expedition. After the Lewis and Clark expedition, fur trappers and traders soon started going into the new territory and later, in the 1830s, the pioneers started going west in their wagon trains. And that brings us to Finn and Ginny's adventure.

This book is slightly different from the others in this series because although the incidents that happen in the story really did happen to real-life pioneers, Finn and Ginny did not follow the journey of one particular set of immigrants. Instead, their adventures are a combination of stories from different wagon trains. To prepare for this book, I read numerous first-hand accounts of emigrant trail pioneers and selected interesting incidents from various accounts. So while all of the adventures that happen to Finn and Ginny really did happen to real emigrant trail pioneers, they didn't happen all on one wagon train. The only exception is Finn's amnesia, though there were accounts of people falling from horses.

Most of the incidents happened exactly as written, but some of them were compiled from various stories. One of them, the runaway train story, is a combination of incidents from different journals. The man riding by with the bells and causing a stampede is from one journal. No wagons were damaged in that particular wagon train stampede, though people were killed and wagons damaged in others. The broken wagon and how they fixed it is from another journal.

Another incident that was compiled from a number of stories was the one about taking the wagon down a steep hill. Steep hills were a hazard that occurred at various points in the pioneers' journey.

A third incident that was a compilation was Benjamin's death from cholera. Many pioneers died from cholera on the trail west, including children, so I made up the story of Benjamin to illustrate their deaths.

I should probably also mention that I have no idea if covering an ox's eyes will calm it down. I know that it works with other animals, but I did not find that particular item in any of the pioneer journals that I read.

Like the other incidents in this book, the "turn back" story really did happen, but not at the point in the trail it happened on in this book. It happened near the California/Oregon border on a branch of the trail that Finn and Ginny weren't on. Also, only one man was doing the scouting and heard the voice.

The story of the wagon that tipped over in the water also happened, but at a different point on the trail.

Finn, Ginny, and their parents are fictitious characters, as are the Campbells, Captain John and his family, Ginny's friend Sarah, the boys who help Finn when he falls from his horse, and Benjamin (mentioned on the previous page). The rest of the people from the nineteenth century mentioned in this book were real people. In the previous *Our America* books, the ancestors Finn and Ginny meet in the story were also my ancestors. Unfortunately, I have no ancestors who went as far as Oregon on the emigrant trail. My ancestors, Alexander Bain (Uncle Alexander) and his family who Finn and Ginny meet at the beginning of the book, stopped their journey in Nebraska. Because I wanted to include the Bains in the story, Finn and Ginny's route at the beginning of their journey is a little awkward. I wanted to include the story of the Elkhorn River flood, but to get to that point after leaving the Bains at Camp Creek, they needed to travel north a bit farther than they probably would have in real life.

While this book is mostly based on accounts told by the people who actually lived through the events in the story, we don't know what their actual conversations were. This means that while most of the incidents in this book actually happened, the conversations associated with them are fictitious, though the content of some of them is taken from various journals. And of course, people in the nineteenth century did not use the same speech patterns that we use today. I chose to write the book using modern speech patterns to make it easier for the young reader.

My goal in this book was to show the hardships the pioneers went through to settle our country. I hope my readers will come away from this book with an appreciation of all that our ancestors went through to give us the life we have today.

Partial Bibliography

Emigrant Trail Travel Journals

Diary of Jane Gould in 1862
By Jane Gould
Webb Research Group Publishers, 1987
Medford, Oregon

Ox-Team Days on the Oregon Trail
By Ezra Meeker & Howard R. Driggs, 1922

Best of Covered Wagon Women
By Kenneth L. Holmes & Michael L. Tate
University of Oklahoma Press, 2008

Reminiscences of a Pioneer
By Colonel William Thompson
San Francisco, 1912

Emigrant Diaries and Journals
The Oregon Territory and Its Pioneers Website
http://www.oregonpioneers.com/diaries.htm

Other Books about the Emigrant Trail

The Prairie Traveler
By Randolph B. Marcy
Originally published in 1859

The Great Platte River Road
By Merrill J. Mattes
University of Nebraska Press

Praise for Susan Kilbride's
Science Unit Studies for Homeschoolers and Teachers

If you are looking for quality science units, but simply don't have the time to put a unit together, Susan's book is perfect for you. If you want to supplement your existing science program, I definitely recommend taking a close look at the book. Those of you who might be a little scared of trying to put together your own science lessons for fear you might get something wrong, fear no more. . . .
Jackie from Quaint Scribbles

This collection of fun science lessons and activities are designed to offer hands on experiments that will satisfy the curious nature of children, while making it easier for parents to teach science.
Kathy Davis of HomeschoolBuzz.com

If you're looking for a science unit study homeschool program that is easy to use and is comprehensive and worth using, then you should check out Science Unit Studies for Homeschoolers and Teachers. *I recently read through the book and really liked what I saw.*
Heidi Johnson of Homeschool-how-to.com

. . . .the conversational style and logical, easy-to-follow instructions certainly make this a recommended and useful tool for any parent; especially those who may be uncomfortable or unfamiliar with teaching science.
Jeanie Frias of California Homeschooler

You make learning science fun!
Brianna, homeschooler, age 10

I think Science Unit Studies for Homeschoolers and Teachers *is a good value and provides a lot of fun, hands-on science for homeschoolers.*
Courtney Larson, The Old Schoolhouse® Magazine

The wealth of information included therein is amazing and the material is novice friendly. I would definitely recommend Science Unit Studies for Homeschoolers and Teachers.
Bridgette Taylor with Hearts at Home Curriculum

Susan's book is full of so many activities that one would have a very full study of general science over the course of a school year if every activity were completed. I teach a General Science class at a local homeschool co-op and I am implementing a lot of the activities in this book into my class this year. There are even short quizzes (complete with answer keys) provided for the older student unit studies. The quizzes are multiple choice in format and cover the main points students should glean from each unit. I highly recommend this book for any science teacher or student. It really makes the teaching of science quite simple and fun. Overall I give Susan's book 5+ stars.
Heart of the Matter Online

We used Science Unit Studies for Homeschoolers and Teachers *at home as part of our homeschooling science lessons. The directions were easy to follow and I loved that they used materials that could be purchased from the grocery store. My children, ages 5, 7, and 9, became excited about learning science, actually jumping up and down when it was time to start science lessons!*
Ilya Perry, homeschooling mother of three with a degree in elementary education

Made in the USA
San Bernardino, CA
12 July 2014